WHEN YOU CAN'T LET GO 3

DAMAGED LOVE SERIES BOOK 3

MIA BLACK

D1528291

CHAPTER 1

Jericka

"Wow, what a surprise," I said to myself out loud. After my initial shock wore off, I opened the door to the hotel room and stepped to the side to let Marco in.

He walked into the room slowly, looking handsome as ever in a pair of jeans and a matching denim jacket. His jet black dreads were long and healthy looking. He wasn't smiling but he had a friendly look in his eyes and a cute smirk on his face. I looked down and saw that he had his hands full. He was carrying a large bouquet of flowers in one hand a huge brown teddy bear in the other. I assumed both of them were for me cause I couldn't have imagined him just riding around with all that for no reason.

I didn't know if I was having a moment of weakness or maybe it was new strength when I'd called Marco earlier. He was doing so much for me that I wanted him to know how greatly appreciated it was. Marco was a real stand up dude and so far he hadn't done or said anything that made it seem like he had another motive for trying to do what he was doing for me; and he was doing a lot.

Marco was still a mystery to me but I planned on using some time that night to try and figure him out some more. He'd come into the strip club where I worked one night and he'd become attracted to me on some crazy shit after only a little while. He threw mad money in my direction when I hit the stage and when we went to the back to talk, he really took the time to talk to me like I was a real person and not just some stripper bitch like most dudes though I was. Marco had offered to help me and my son Jasheem out, no strings attached. At first I'd turned him down but when shit went left with my man

Hov and I had to make an exit, Marco had been there to help me out in a major way. He'd come through with the hotel room and now he was coming through with something else.

"Wassup?" Marco greeted me.

He handed me the flowers and the teddy bear and then reached in for a hug. My hands were full then but I leaned in and hugged him. I couldn't even try and play it off; the smile on my face was going from ear to ear. I was happy as hell to see him and even to get the gifts from him. It had been so long since Hov had brought anything into the house besides headaches or even the damn mail.

"Hey, what's going on?" I greeted him as we hugged. "Thanks for this. You didn't have to get me anything. You've already done enough for me."

"Nah, it's no problem," he said to me.

It was late as hell, or early, depending on how you looked at it. Marco didn't seem tired at all though. He also smelled fresh like he'd just taken a shower or something. I eyed him as he entered the room. He had on a pair of jean pants with a matching jacket and a white shirt underneath. It was a simple outfit but it fight him just right. He had swag, that was for sure.

I invited him in and closed the door behind him. He walked into the room and I showed him to the bedroom area. He headed to the other bed, the empty one, and sat down on the corner. I sat down across from him on my bed. I wasn't trying to lead him one but that had been where I was at before he'd come back to the room.

"What you been up to?" I asked him. For as much as Marco was doing for me, I still didn't know too much about him. A lot of him was still very much a mystery to me but I hoped that as he and I got closer and clicked more that we'd be able to really get to know one another on some real shit. I still didn't know what I was doing with Marco but I was just gonna go along with the ride.

"Just been handlin' some business," he said to me. "I got a lot of shit goin' on," he said. "But what you been up to? Oh peep this, look what else I got you." He reached into the inside of his jacket and pulled out a bottle of champagne. He must not have been holding on to it too long cause it was still ice cold as I took it from his hands.

Marco didn't know it but thanks to my best friend Tamika, I knew a lot more about what business he was handling than he probably thought. It wasn't any info that I could do anything with but I liked to be informed about things so I made it my business to ask questions when I got the chance to.

"I ain't been doin' nothin'," I said. I walked over to the other side of the room and held the bottle away from me in my outstretched arm. I'd opened a lot of champagne bottles but my ass was always afraid whenever I did it.

"Just put it with ya' thumb," Marco said with a little laugh. He was enjoying himself even through my fear.

I pushed up on the top of the bottle with my thumb and the cork went flying across the room and hit the door. A little of it spilled out the bottle and onto the carpet but not too much. I raised the bottle to my mouth and sipped some of it to stop it from spilling. My nose tickled.

I didn't have any champagne glasses so I poured the champagne into the two cups I did have. I handed one to Hov and kept the other.

"I wish I had glasses for this but I gotta use what I got," I said as I sat back down.

"To get what you want?" he said with a laugh.

I joined in with his laughter. "I love that quote," I said to him. "The Players Club is one of my favorite movies."

"Me too," he said, still smiling.

I held up my glass to my lips and he stopped me. "What?" I asked him.

"We gotta toast," he said. "You can't just drink champagne. You gotta toast." He held his glass up in the air, waiting for mine to join it.

"It's been awhile since I had something to toast to," I said in a sad tone. I glanced at myself in the mirror, checking out my cuts and bruises. I looked up at him, making sure to stare him in his eyes. I wanted to make sure he knew that I was serious about what I was saying to him. "Marco, I really wanna let you know that I appreciate everything that you doing for me and my son. You haven't even met my baby yet and you tryin to help us out. It means a lot to me."

He nodded his head at me. "It's nothin," he said. "Actually, let's toast to that. To your new start."

"To my new start," I said. I held up my glass and clinked it with his and took a sip of the champagne. I hoped that our little toast held some weight to somebody and that it really did mean a new start for me and Jah.

He poured us out another glass of champagne. I didn't have a buzz yet but I knew that something would probably be kicking in soon enough, especially since I hadn't eaten. We sat and sipped the champagne and I was surprised cause it was Marco that was trying to keep the conversation going. He was asking me all about me and I liked it.

"How you end up workin' the pole?" Marco asked me. "No disrespect or anything."

"We needed money," I said to him. "None taken either." It was true. I saw the end long before that shit came when I first found out that Hov was using. Once he hit the point where he was lying about his use, I knew that the writing was on the wall. We got kicked out of where we lived and ended up having to move to the place we were at then.

"Did he...you know...did he make you go out there?" Marco asked. It was funny to watch him be so awkward and stuff. I knew it had to be a weird conversation for someone to be having though.

"Nah," I said. "Hov ain't the pimp type." I laughed at the thought of it. The funny and sad thing about it was that though Hov wasn't pimping me out, that nigga sure was collecting my money like he was.

"Oh, ok," he said.

"Nah, it was me that came up with it. Hov was against it at first but once I showed him how far behind we were on the bills, we figured out it was probably the best thing to do," I explained.

"Why ain't you let that nigga get a job?" Marco asked. The look on his face made it clear that he ain't really approve too much of Hov. He was far from the only one in that club.

"It wasn't about me *letting* him," I said with a little attitude. "It was about what was going on at the time. People are real quick to judge my situation but I'm the one living it. Hov was getting worse, Jasheem was getting older. Looking back, I see that I had two options but when I was younger and in the mess, I only saw one way out that meant keeping my family together and that was what I chose. It ain't pretty but it's my story."

Marco nodded his head in approval. "Nah, I don't blame you," he said to me. "Honestly speaking, God forbid I end up addicted to something, but if I was, I'd want a shorty like you by my side holdin' me down. But I'd get better. I wouldn't wanna be out there on that shit like that."

"It's not a good place to be," I said. "And besides, I'm through holding niggas down. The next dude I get with gotta be able to support me just as equally as I support him. No negotiations."

"That's how it should be," he said. "I'm gonna hold down my next shorty for real." He eyed me up and down.

Marco was something else. I was still trying to figure him out but I figured that time would allow us to get to know each other better. I was excited to see what the future held though.

"Tell me about you," I said to Marco. I already had a lot of background information on him thanks to Tamika but I wanted to hear it from his mouth. Marco had been talking and showing a good game since all this started and it seemed like he was trying to build with me but I needed to know him for real. I wasn't expecting for him to give me the whole breakdown of his life but I wanted to know more.

He looked at me with a strange look in his eyes and then just smiled at me. "What you wanna know? I'm a regular nigga. I just got out the lock up and shit not too long ago. I'm here handling some business," he explained to me.

"What line of work you in?" I asked him. I wasn't trying to be nosey but I wanted to see how far he planned on letting me in.

"I think you can figure that out," he said to me. I nodded my head to let him know that I understood him. "Yeah, so that's me. I do a lot. I'm out here tryin' to take over and shit. The funny shit is that I ain't even know who you was when I met you." He chuckled.

"What you mean? I ain't nobody," I said to him.

"That's true and not true all at the same time," he said. "I'm a smart dude. I wasn't about to pull up in a new city and not know who the players are. That's stupid. I heard all about that nigga Hov while I was locked up and shit but I ain't know you was his girl."

I eyed him suspiciously. "Does that matter?" I was feeling a little uneasy. Maybe I'd been misjudging Marco. He could have some other motive or something.

"Nah, not at all," he said to me and held up his hands up in a gesture of peace. "We hear everything on the inside so after that nigga fell off, we heard about it too. I ain't goin' after that nigga or nothing, no disrespect, but he ain't the man no more so he don't really matter. It's just funny that you and I met."

I felt better about the situation then. I wasn't trying to be a pawn in some street game between them at all. Marco seemed like he was telling the truth too. If he had some plan to try and hurt Hov through me, he'd already had mad chances to make a move and hadn't. I figured he was cool and he and I meeting each other was just a coincidence. Not to mention that what he'd said was very true; Hov's name held no weight. He was young but he'd let his name lose its street value.

"Word, it's funny how stuff works itself out sometimes," I said. "If I wouldn't have met you, I don't know what my ass would have done. I would've probably gone to my mother's house but Hov would have probably shown up there and caused a scene."

"Don't let these lames stress you out," Marco said.

I wanted to know more about him so I asked the question had been on my mind for a little while. "So why you single?" I asked him. Marco hadn't said at that point whether or not he was but if he was putting me and my kid up in a hotel room, I was pretty sure that he didn't have a bitch somewhere waiting for him to come home.

"I gotta find the right one," he said to me. His eyes seemed to glow in the dim light of the hotel room. He looked me up and down and licked his brown, full lips. I had to shift my legs a little bit cause I was feeling horny.

"I feel you," I said in a seductive way. I licked my lips too. I wanted him to know that I'd picked up on his little flirtation that he'd throw my way. "But I'm surprised no chick out here tried to lock you down. You got kids or anything?"

"Nah, no kids over here. I want some one day though," he explained to me. "My brother and I are close, even though that nigga locked up. I want my kids to have siblings and shit. I

don't want them growin' up alone but ain't
nothing wrong with that.

"I feel you," I said. My brother Jayson and I
had been close growing up and were still close to
one another. He was younger than me but made
it clear that he was the man of our household
and was always willing to fight to defend me or
our mother. I knew a lot of siblings that didn't
get along but my brother and I weren't like that
at all. I wanted the same for Jasheem too. He
should know what it's like to have someone call
you big brother. "I want another one too."

It felt strange to be admitting my desire to
have more kids to Marco because it was something that I'd wanted to say to Hov for a while. I
really did want to have another baby with him
and we'd been trying right before his ass started
doing drugs. It was such a weird thing to be able
to spot the exact moment that your life took a
turn for the worse. We stopped trying for more
kids but the feeling never really left me. I wanted
to have a big family but I had to put that out of
my head cause I had other shit to worry about.

"Oh word? Another boy or a girl this time?"
Marco asked. I liked that he was genuinely
curious about my plans and stuff.

"It don't matter to me as long as it's healthy," I said. "Ten fingers, ten toes, and a healthy heartbeat. But if I had to choose, I'd probably want a little girl."

"Yeah, a girl would be cool," he said.

"I'm surprised you don't want a little boy," I said. "You know...someone to carry on your family name and all that other shit." Most guys usually wanted boys. When I was pregnant with Jah, Hov had made it clear that he was hoping for a little boy. He even picked out Jasheem's name from a list that we'd narrowed it down to.

"Nah, don't get me wrong, I'm like you with the healthy stuff. I don't care as long as the baby comes out good. But I feel like I'd do good with a little girl," he explained to me.

"Why's that?" I asked. I was curious then.

"I just feel like I'd take care of her the right way. I see a lot of bitches out here in my line of work and shit and it's so clear that they ain't had no daddies around when they was growing up. When I have a little girl, she ain't gonna want for shit. That way she can choose who she wanna be with and don't gotta rely on a nigga for nothin," he said.

I nodded my head in agreement. A lot of

what he was saying definitely described my mindset. I'd been proving to myself for a while that I'd be good with or without Hov. I just didn't realize it though. "That's how I feel it should be, for a boy or a girl," I said to him. "My mother raised my brother and I to *both* know how to do everything around the house, cook, clean, all that. She also made sure we never had to ask anyone but her for anything. That's how I'm raising Jasheem." I smiled just thinking about my baby.

"You a good mother," Marco said to me. It wasn't a question, it was a statement. It was like he'd been debating on it for a while but had finally come to his conclusion about it.

"Thank you," I said. "But you ain't even meet Jasheem yet." I laughed a little bit.

"I don't need to. I can just te—" Marco stopped talking. Someone was knocking at the door.

Marco looked at me suspiciously and I just made a face showing my own confusion. I hadn't told anyone besides my mother that I was even at a hotel so I didn't know who it was knocking. It was definitely way too early for it to be the cleaning service or anything so I was confused. I was more nervous than I should have been but there was every chance that Hov had followed me from the club to the hotel. I could see him doing it too, especially if he was still high.

Marco stood up and reached into his jacket. He reached behind his back and pulled out a 9 millimeter. I knew it because I used to carry one around with me for protection. I wasn't afraid to use it either. I'd gone to the gun range a couple of times and I had good aim.

Marco held his finger up to his mouth and silently told me to be quiet. He walked over to the door with his hand behind his back. He looked through the peephole.

"Who is it?" He asked.

"Room service," I heard a male voice from the other side of the door say.

Marco unlocked the door and asked the guy what the room service was for. He nodded his head and allowed the guy to bring a tray into the room. He tipped him and then locked the door behind him.

"What's that?" I asked him. I was mad confused.

"My bad," he said with a smile on his face,

"I forgot I got this for you as a surprise." Marco opened the top of the tray and underneath it was a bottle of champagne on ice and one of those fruit platters with all types of fruits covered in chocolate: strawberries, apples, pineapples, bananas, melons, everything.

I busted out laughing and then stood up and walked over to the middle of the room where the tray was. I grabbed a piece of the strawberry and slowly put it into my mouth in a seductive way. I eyed Marco again and he was getting what I was throwing in his direction.

CHAPTER 2

Hov

Staying at Kia's house for a couple of days was cool but I felt like that white bitch Dorothy from *The Wizard of Oz*, cause there was no place like home. I missed my crib. I missed my lady. I missed my son. It was just simple things that I really wanted back. I just wanted to be back in my own crib, laying with Jericka and Jasheem while we watched some movie or something. It was those moments that I needed the most cause in those times when we ain't worry about nothing; bills, the streets, nothing. Shit was good. But that had all changed.

Not to downplay Kia or anything. I couldn't front, Kia definitely knew how to treat me right. She was definitely working real hard to try and make me stay. All I had to do was mention Jericka and Kia found some way to make shit better for me. Every time we smoked, we fucked. She'd even suck my dick sometimes just cause. It was like she couldn't get enough or like she had something prove.

The thing was though, Kia's house wasn't my home, no matter how much she tried to make it be. I wasn't trying to make it that either. I knew that when I did what I did to Jericka that I'd fucked up. I wanted to talk to her for real. I really wanted to talk to Jasheem more though.

Being as high as I was, I honestly don't know what the fuck I would have done if I had been able to get into his room that day. I never wanted him to see me and Jericka fighting so I was shocked when little man came out of his room. The last thing I was expecting him to do was throw that iPad at me. He must've really been going through it. I knew he had to be mad at me cause all he saw was me hurting his mother.

I wanted to sit Jasheem down and let him know that what he saw me doing was wrong and that he should never do that to any woman. I also wanted to let him know that I was his father and he needed to respect me. That iPad shit had me tight still.

The thing was though, I couldn't have a conversation with Jericka or Jah unless Jericka stopped acting up and hit me up. I'd tried hitting her up a couple of times since that day but she hadn't responded at all. I left her voicemails and I knew she got them cause her box was never full.

"Hov," said Kia one morning. I'd just gotten out the shower and was in my towel gettin' dressed in her bedroom. She had been getting on my nerves the day before so I was trying to avoid her ass.

"Yeah?" I responded. I looked at my phone and saw that it was only ten in the morning. It was too early for her to be nagging about something so I hoped that wasn't why she was calling my name.

"My stash getting low," she announced. She looked at me like that was supposed to mean something to me. Her eyes had gotten a little wide and she raised her eyebrows.

I just looked at her and shook my head. "Ok, and?" I asked. I didn't know why she was telling me. That was her problem, not mine. I was gonna find a way to get high regardless. I knew she'd let me come back to her crib so it ain't even matter too much to me.

"What you mean *and?*" She asked me. She looked a little annoyed. This was why I just needed to be back in my own crib. I could deal with Jericka but I wasn't down to learn some new bitch all over again. "You helped me smoke it all. So look, I need some money to get some more."

"Where am I gettin' money from, Kia?" I asked her. "You let me know. Cause last time I checked, the cops are probably lookin' for me for the shit with Jericka."

"You can do something for money though, Hov," Kia said to me. The look on her face told me that she was prepared to argue with me regardless of what I said so it didn't even matter to me

"Aight," I said to her. I *definitely* wasn't tryin' to

give Kia any money for drugs. I could have kept my own money and just bought my own shit. The only issue was that I wasn't tryin' to be seen on the streets like that. I had one case against me already and I was sure that Jericka was pressing charges on me. James told me that he'd been walkin' past my crib and spotted a cop car outside. It might not have been for me but somethin' told me that I needed to be on the lookout.

"What does that mean?" Kia asked.

"Yo, I hear you," I said to her in an aggressive way. Kia seemed to take the hint then. She rolled her eyes and got up, heading for the living room. I was glad too. I was annoyed with looking at her at the moment.

If Kia was about to start asking me for money and shit, maybe it was time for me to start making my way back to my own crib. I hadn't planned on being at Kia's for too long anyway so it just made sense anyway. On top of all of that, I missed Jericka and I missed my son.

I put my underwear on and sat on the side of the bed. I pulled my phone out of my jean pocket and scrolled till I found Jericka's number and dialed it.

While the phone rang, I hoped that she'd

pick up. It was early enough that she was probably still up. I knew that if she wasn't home then she was probably at her mother's house. I thought about driving by there but I wasn't about to try and make shit worse, at least not yet. Shit, I honestly hoped Jericka had calmed down so I could get some money from her. She didn't answer the first time and it went to her voicemail.

I didn't leave a message, but I did hang up and call right back. It rang and rang and went to voicemail. I decided to just leave her a message. I hoped she'd listen to it and just call me back. I wanted to talk to her to try and smooth shit over with us.

"Wassup baby, it's me. I'm sorry for what happened before. I was high. Mad high. But you know I never wanna hurt you, never on purpose. Can you drop the charges Jericka? I'm ready to fix what I broke. I know it was me who fucked it all up but I need you and Jah. That's the only way I'm gonna heal. I just want my family back baby. I can go to rehab and all that. Oh look, I parked you car in the lot over by 41st. It's safe. You can go to them people and get the spare. I just wanna talk when you ready.

I love you," I said. I had to say that shit mad quick. I was surprised they hadn't cut me off when I was trying to talk.

I thought about getting dressed but the truth was that I ain't have nowhere to go. I laid back on the bed and put my hand behind my head. I hoped Jericka called me back.

CHAPTER 3

Jericka

Marco and I chilled in the hotel room and talked for what seemed like forever. We finished the bottle of champagne he bought and had gone halfway through the second one. He was sitting on the other bed looking fine as hell. I was feeling kind of tipsy, no doubt a symptom of the liquor. I hadn't eaten any dinner so it was just some expensive champagne on an empty stomach which wasn't a good combination.

Marco and I sat up for a little while longer and watched some TV. That didn't last too long though since we were both tired as hell. I climbed into my bed and got under the covers. Much to my surprise, Marco climbed into the other bed.

I had to admit it, a bitch was shocked by that. I knew that he wanted me but he was also making it clear to me that he was just trying to be a gentleman. I decided that if that was that he wanted, I'd try and listen to him. I asked him if he minded the TV being off sand he said no so I turned it off. We turned the lights out and laid in the darkness.

I was only wearing a pair of boy shirts and a tank top. I kept clothes at the club and in my car cause I liked to have options, plus if something got dirty I wanted backups.

Laying there alone, I couldn't help but to start to feel lonely. For like ten minutes I tossed and turned, trying to get comfortable but I couldn't find a spot. Between the liquor having me antsy and the bed just not feeling right, I couldn't find my groove. I figured out just then what it was that I needed. It was the thing that I was scared of but also really wanted to try out all at the same time. I was feeling something new but I wasn't sure of what it was.

Silently, I slipped out of my bed. I threw my

covers off of me and slid out. My feet hit the soft, carpeted floor. Just as quick as I'd slipped out of my bed, I'd climbed into Marco's with him. He must have been sleeping cause he sounded a little surprised. He let out a little groan when I got in with him. It wasn't anger though, just the surprise. He was laying on his back which was exactly what I was hoping for. His body felt warm next to mine as I snuggled up to him. He had on a pair of basketball shorts and no shirt. His body felt rock hard next to mine, ripping with all those muscles. He was so damned handsome.

I laid my head on his chest and he wrapped his arm around me. I laid there, feeling safer in his arms then I'd felt in forever. I took in his scent and he smelled good as hell even closer. Marco and I fell asleep just like that after he kissed me on the forehead.

Now, the night before might have been the fairytale part but the morning after was the real thing. My mother used to say that to Jayson and I all the time when we were growing you. "You need to see what people look like in the morning and then decide if you wanna be wit' 'em," she'd say to us.

Marco could do whatever he wanted the night before to be a gentleman but when I woke up a couple of hours later, he was just a man. Morning wood had hit Marco something crazy. He was still handsome as fuck, no crust around the lips and stuff, thankfully. He'd moved a lot in his sleep and I don't know the shit was intentional or not but somehow his basketball shorts had come down and the covers were only covering me.

Marco was still laying on his back a wearing a pair of black boxer briefs. His dick was semi hard and looked like it was struggling to get out. It looked like a monster too. I couldn't tell how many inches long it was, but it was thick. I ran to the bathroom and brushed my teeth before I came back out and got back into bed. I did a quick little rinse down there in case it went that far. I had to be ready. He was still sleeping thankfully.

I was careful as I reached into his shorts and pulled his dick out. It was big in my hands and was nice looking too. I started to jerk it up and down a little bit just to get it all the way hard. At its full length, it was easily nine solid inches. It was bigger than Hov, that was for sure and that was crazy cause Hov was packing. It was weird to be doing what I was doing. I'd never cheated on Hov, not the entire time we'd been together. I'd seen my fair share of dicks cause of Tamika and the fact that niggas loved her, but I hadn't really done shit with anyone else besides Hov. I knew I was ready though. Something in me felt like it was guiding me and I was just going along with it.

Strangely enough, one place that shit with Hov and I always seemed to click was the bedroom. He always made it clear to me that I was the best he'd ever been with. It was a gift and a curse at times to hear that, cause to me, he was special for being me only but for him, I was one among a few. I pushed that shit out of my mind though. I wanted to do what I was about to do to Marco with a clear mind and thinking about Hov was the exact opposite of that.

I put my mouth in the tip of his dick. It was like a baseball bat, thin at the top and thicker at the bottom. I slowly slid my mouth down onto it, trying to see how far I could go. I closed my mouth and the let the spit fill my mouth as I went up and down on it. He was circumcised which I liked cause I ain't have the time to be peeling no bananas.

After a couple of seconds of me going up and down, Marco's eyes burst open. He looked surprised, then happy. A sleepy grin went across his face. He closed his eyes and just let me keep going.

For the next few minutes I went back to work on his dick. I built a rhythm and found out that I could take a lot more of it into my mouth than I thought. After a while, Marco had to drop his whole fake sleeping routine cause it was feeling good. He let out a couple of moans and curse words and I knew that I was puttin' it on him for real.

"Damn yo," he said. He licked his lips and sat up to look at me. I didn't stop sucking his dick but I looked up at him. Hov loved it when I did that and Marco did too. He licked his lips and tried to put his hand on my head but I moved it away and kept going at my own rhythm. He wasn't in control; I was.

He was a lot taller than me but with us laying in the bed, I was able to use that to my advantage. I stopped sucking his dick and slowly slithered up his body like I was a snake. I got face to face with him and was about to kiss him but he ran to the bathroom to slay his morning dragon breath. I was glad for that too. I couldn't stand a nigga with no hygiene.

Marco came back and moved me so I was laying on my back. He'd slipped out of his underwear and was now naked in front of me. He climbed onto the bed and slid down some so he was face first with my pussy. He put his big hands on my thighs and grabbed on tightly. Marco pulled me onto him. His whole face disappeared between my legs.

I moaned in a way that even shocked me. I'd had my pussy eaten mad times before but never like that. Marco had dove right into me like he was a swimmer at the Olympics. His tongue and fingers were moving around inside of me like he was trying to explore every part of it.

"Oh...Marco," I moaned his name.

He kept on rubbing my whole body. He caressed my thighs. He palmed my ass cheeks. He grabbed my breasts and played with them. It felt so damn good.

"Damn yo," he said in between licks, "I ain't know your skin was soft like this." He couldn't

get enough of grabbing onto me. I was loving it
for real.

I sat up a little bit and reached out for his
head. I was trying to push him away. I was on
the verge of a real orgasm like I don't think I'd
had before. I'd had sex before but this was some
other shit. My whole body felt different. As I
tried to push him away, I felt it happen like that
shit ain't never happen before. My whole body
shook with an orgasm so intense that my legs
closed up like a vice grip around Marco's face. I
let out a sound that was half a yell and half a
moan. I was glad that he'd gotten a room that
was so big cause if we were closer to the door
that led to outside that someone would have
heard us. I then I laid back down on the bed,
breathing hard like I'd just run a fucking
marathon.

"Yeah, that nigga don't take care of you,"
Marco said. He sounded like a doctor giving
someone some bad news. "We can stop if you
want. You seem like you a little tired."

I'd been laying there with my eyes closed but
I opened them and looked at him. That nigga
had the nerve to be smiling like something was
funny. If he wanted a challenge, he was about to

get one. I may not have had as many bodies as other people but I wasn't some stuck up bitch or something.

"Get a condom," I said to him. Marco was there thinking that I was playing with him. I get it...it had been a while...if ever, that I'd had an orgasm that intense, but I wasn't about to tap out. I was a stripper. I sold fantasies. Now I was about to act one out.

Marco slipped the condom on himself and I told him to lay down on his back. I straddled him and started to lick and suck on his neck. I was making sure the shit was extra sexy. I kept flipping my hair back and forth in a sexy ass way. I licked, sucked, and bit as his neck. I put his hands on my titties and made him play with them. I was making him feel like he was in control.

And then I flipped it on him.

I slid my body up and down his until I was in the perfect position. With both legs over his abdomen I moved down a little bit till I was right over his dick. , I took all of his inches into me, slowly, but without stopping. It was a little difficult at first cause he was so thick but I got the hang of it. I rode Marco like nobody's business. I moved my hips back and forth on him and was glad that he could keep up...at first. After a while Marco was asking me to slow down and shit. When he came, he sat up and kissed me deep on the lips. He grabbed me in his arms and we just stayed there kissing for the next few minutes.

He went to the bathroom to get cleaned up. When he came back, I went in there and by the time I came out, he was knocked. I climbed into bed next to him and drifted off to sleep.

"Jericka…" Someone was shaking me. I felt a hand on my shoulder. I didn't know how long I'd been asleep. I got shook again.

"What?" I asked. I opened my eyes and Marco was in front of me on the other bed. Next to the bed was another room service tray. This time it had breakfast one it; bacon, eggs, whole wheat toast, orange juice, water, and a nice looking fruit salad.

I sat up in the bed. I looked at the clock by the bed and saw that it was still early. I had a little bit before I needed to be at my mother's house. I hoped Jasheem was tired cause I needed a nap.

"My bad, but I got breakfast. I know you

gotta get your son so I ain't want you to over-sleep," Marco explained. He was sitting across from me in his white t-shirt and jeans. He looked like he'd showered while I was sleeping. He'd tied his long dreads up into a ponytail behind his head.

"Thank you," I said to him. I sat up in the bed, wrapping the sheets around my still naked body. I asked him if he was hungry but he told me to just make my plate first. I was tired but also hungry so I had a plate with a little of everything on it. Marco did too.

We sat in silence for a little bit but Marco spoke and I could tell by the look on his face that he'd been thinking about it for a while.

"Yo, I wanna talk to you about somethin'," he said to me.

"Alright," I said. I put down the piece of toast I had in my hand.

"I want you to get with me," he said. His face was still kind of blank so I couldn't really read him. I really didn't know what to say.

"Wait. I—" I said but he interrupted.

"Chill, chill," he said to me with a slight smirk. He was showing off that same confidence that I liked in him. You had to respect a dude that moved like he was always in control. "I'm not talkin 'bout right this second or even today. I'm just sayin'...it's what I want. You gotta leave this nigga that's beating on you before he kills you. And if you tell me it's not a possibility, you lying."

Marco's words were true. I couldn't lie to myself and say that the thought that Hov might kill me one day hadn't crossed my mind. When he was high, he was a different dude all the way around. I didn't know what to expect. Sometimes he'd get high and violent. But there would be times where Hov would get high and just wanna cuddle with me and tell me how he loved me. There would be times where he'd talk about the future and what he wanted for us. I wanted to believe that either of them was the real Hov but I was sure they weren't.

"Yeah, you right," I said to him. I really did hate to admit it but it was the truth. Marco deserved that at least.

"I got a spot you could live in," he said to me. He must have seen the look on my face when he said that. "But I know you not ready for that. I'm down to help you get your own crib though. A two bedroom for you and your son. I wanna meet him. I know I'm gonna love 'em like he's my own." Marco paused. I didn't know where all that shit was coming from but it seemed like he'd already put a lot of thought into it. "Jericka, on some serious shit, I could see myself with you. If you get wit' me, you wouldn't have to worry 'bout goin' back to no strip club or nothin like that. I wanna give you everything you used to have a more. I can treat you like a queen."

The look in Marco's eyes was a sincere one. He meant every word of what he was saying. I had to admit that it sounded nice. I hated to be one of those people, but I always thought that if something seemed too good to be, it probably was.

"Marco, I like what you saying. I just think we should sit and talk about it for a little bit," I said to him.

"I feel you. I just——" he stopped talking cause his phone rang. He answered it and listened to it for a little while. He told someone to call someone else and then call him back.

"My bad," he said. "I gotta go. I know it's early but the streets is callin'."

"I know how that is," I said to him.

"I'm bout to head out," he said as he stood up and threw on the rest of his clothes. He reached into his wallet and pulled out two crisp $100 bills and handed them to me. "That's for you," he said.

"Thanks," I said as I took the money from him. It was definitely appreciated.

"I can come back here later if you want," he said to me.

"Yeah, that'd be cool," I said.

"Aight," he said. "After I'm done hustlin' I'll be back."

"OK, cool," I said. We both walked over to the door of the hotel room.

"Can a nigga get a hug?" Marco asked. He turned and looked at me with puppy dog eyes as he asked.

"Of course," I said. I had to tiptoe just a little bit but I held him tight before he walked out the door.

I turned around and walked back over to my bed. I laid in it and grabbed my phone. I'd turned the vibration and sound off the night before. I didn't wanna be disturbed when I was with Marco.

My mother had called me, of course.

Tamika had text me to ask how I was doing. I made a note to try and link with her later on that day. I saw that Hov had called me and left a voicemail for a change. I usually didn't check my voicemails but I saw that it was kind of long so I decided to listen.

I listened to Hov's entire message and then replayed it again. Wow, he sounded so sad. I hadn't heard him be that sad in God only knew how long. It would be typical Hov shit though for him to all of a sudden start feeling bad right when he knew he'd fucked up the most. I wondered if the cops were out looking for him. I tried to shake the sound of his voice from my head.

I got up and took my clothes, headed to the bathroom to take a shower. I turned the water on and it took me a while to find the perfect temperature but once I found it I was ready. I took a nice, long, hot shower. I tried to wash away all the shit I had on my mind but it wasn't that easy to put Hov and his words in the back of mind.

When I got out the shower I was snapped back to reality though. I wrapped my towel around my body and stood in front of the mirror about to brush my teeth. I stared at my reflection and felt anger and shit swell up inside my chest. I was staring at my face and just imagining how he could claim to love me and do this shit to me.

I was still so torn though. Hov was special to me. I'd be lying if I said otherwise. He was talking on my voicemail about going to rehab and he sounded more sincere than he ever had before. I wanted the old Hov back. I didn't care if that nigga went back to hustling or what. I just wanted the man that I used to know back. I wondered if he was even still inside.

I got dressed and did some heavy thinking. I went back and forth about it more times than I could count. I was trying to figure out every possible angle of the shit but there was just too much to figure out. Hov wanted me to drop the charges against him but I wasn't too sure. I knew that the only way for him to really get help would be for him to go to rehab and he couldn't do that with charges against him, but him going to jail could help him rehab.

I finally decided to just drop the charges. I'd got to the precinct later on and drop them. I wasn't 100% sure about it but the more I thought about it, the better it felt. I wasn't planning on getting back together with Hov, at least not for real, until he'd completed a nice stay in rehab. I couldn't afford to keep letting him get over on me...financially or otherwise.

Hov had really pissed me off with this shit with my car too. I was so damn mad as I went downstairs to catch a cab. I had the cab wait for me while I got a spare, then I had him take me to where my car was parked. I got in my car and drove it to the hotel where I paid for parking and charged it to the room. I drove my mother's car to her house so she could go to work. I was so over all the bullshit. I needed life to settle down.

CHAPTER 4

Hov

It was a little later on in the morning. I was laying down out on the couch while Kia was knocked out in her bedroom. She'd come into the room after I left my voicemail for Jericka. Of course Kia tried to flip it on me and all this shit and I had to check that bitch and remind her that I wasn't her man and I could do what I wanted. Kia was strange though so once I checked her, she got all horny and shit. I fucked her ass right to sleep.

I was flippin' through the channels tryin' to find something to watch but it wasn't shit on. I never understood why niggas paid for cable if they ain't watch like three quarters of the channels there. I ended up throwing on a rerun of Law and Order.

My phone vibrated on the floor. I was gonna ignore it but something told me to just answer it.

"Oh shit," I said out loud. Jericka had text me. I sat up and shit like she was in the room with me or something.

I went and got my car, her message read.

OK. I typed out the message and sent it. *How are u? Wyd?*

We don't gotta do all that, said her message. Damn, she was cold hearted for real. I wondered if she'd only text me just to tell me about the car. My little theory was proven wrong though cause the phone went off in my hand after a couple of seconds. I was nervous as I opened the message.

Look, I'm not tryin to turn this into a long conversation, at least not right now. I'm willing to drop the charges BUT there are conditions. I will only drop them if you go to rehab and STAY CLEAN this time around!! Not to mention that I also want you to go to anger management. You can't ever put your hands on me again and I mean that shit! You need to promise me that. If you want your family back, this is the only way that it's gonna happen Hov. I want Jasheem to grow up with both of his parents in his life but you gotta be willing to do your part if that's gonna happen. This is your last chance to prove you love us more than drugs.

I reread her message twice just to make sure I'd read the shit the right way. Wow, I wasn't expecting that shit at all. Jericka was willing to drop the charges? I couldn't have wished for anything better than that. I wanted to fuckin jump for joy right then. Any other charges on top of the shit I was already facing was just gonna make sure that I ended up going to jail for some real time and I wasn't trying to do that at all.

I took my time and typed out a message to her.

Jericka baby I LOVE U! I promise u that this time ain't like the other times. I wanna be better for me. I know u don't think I be listenin to u but I do. I know that Jah is at that age and he sees the shit that be goin on. I don't want my little man to hate me. He shouldn't have to go through that and neither should u. I wanna go to rehab baby.

I was sincere about the shit I was saying. The only issue with it was that I was saying it just to make Jericka feel better. I knew her like the back of my hand. I'd been with her for too long to not know her. I had to admit that she had pulled out a surprise when she pressed charges. I must've hit her ass too hard.

She was really surprising me though cause I wasn't expecting her response to be what it was.

Hov, I wanna believe you but we done been down this road too many times before. I can't just come runnin back to you and hope that you gonna go to rehab. It's not fair to me or to you. I don't wanna doubt you but if I drop the charges and get back with you, what am I saying to you? That it's ok to do what you did and for me to just get back with you? Nah? You gotta be clean for at least a month. One month at least and then we can start to talk.

"Start to talk?" I mumbled to myself. Who the fuck did Jericka think she was. She was on some next level shit for real. This *definitely* wasn't the answer that I was looking for but there wasn't much else that I could do about it. She could talk tough via text message, but in person Jericka would be eating out the palm of my hand. I still had her wrapped around my finger.

OK, I'm wit it. Whatever it takes. I just want my family back. I want US to be US again. I know we not tryin to link up or anything but can I get a couple of dollars to get to the rehab place? I'm broke but I wanna check in ASAP.

I was being serious about most of the shit I was saying to Jericka, but I ain't really have no intention at all on going to rehab, at least not that day or anytime in the near future. I waited around a couple of minutes, hoping she'd text back soon.

CHAPTER 5

Jericka

My mother was bitching when I got to her house about how I'd gotten there fifteen minutes late. I tried to tell her everything that I had to do before I got to her house but she wasn't trying to hear it. I was especially annoyed cause we sat at her house for a little longer while she finished breakfast. I was all too glad to get out her car when she dropped Jah and I off at the hotel.

We got in the elevator and headed up to our room. I'd been thinking about how to explain it to him cause I knew he'd have questions about what was going on. I needed to run back out and of course he was coming with me but I wanted to talk to him.

"Mommy, why we here? We not goin home?" Jasheem asked me as I closed the door to the hotel room behind us. I showed him over to one of the freshly made beds and told him to climb up and have a seat.

"Jasheem, I wanna talk to you," I said to him. "Do you remember what happened yesterday with mommy and daddy?" I'd been racking my brain for a while trying to figure out which approach would be best. I needed to be delicate cause I knew that this could affect him for the rest of his life.

Tears welled up in his eyes. He held his hands up to wipe them and I rushed over to my baby and grabbed him in my arms. I knew it had to be hurting him just to think about. I couldn't imagine what was going on inside his little head.

"Jasheem, because of what happened, your daddy and I can't be around each other right now so me and you are gonna stay here for a little while," I explained to him.

"Why?" Jasheem asked. He hadn't started

crying all the way but he was sniffling like he might start at any minute.

"Your daddy has some problems...problems that he has to work out on his own. He and I both love you and he's gonna fix his problems and come back," I said to him. I never wanted to be one of them bitter bitches who poisoned their kids about their father. I wanted Jasheem to form his own opinion about Hov but I wasn't gonna act like the truth wasn't true.

"Is he gonna come back to us?" Jasheem asked.

At that point my mother's instinct wanted to take over. I wanted to tell me son that his father was gonna get himself together but I didn't know if I could say it without it being a lie. I'd seen the monster inside of Hov. The drugs might have brought it out of him but it was always lurking below the surface.

"Daddy's gonna come back when he's ready," I said to him. That was the best that I could offer him. I let him go and got down on my knees in front of him. I needed to cheer him up. "It's gonna be different but we're gonna get through it, ok? You still gonna go to grandma's house. You still get to spend all the time you want with me. You gonna be fine. You trust me?"

He nodded his head. I gave him a hug and a kiss. I didn't want to have Jah all worked up over everything that was going on. It was important for him to be a child when he was supposed to be one and I didn't wanna put more on him than he could bare.

I showed Jah around the room and told him that we'd be back in a little bit. We had an errand to run.

We got in my car and we drove to the precinct that was handling my case against Hov. I walked in and asked for the detective handling my case. The officers in there made it clear that they'd rather be anywhere else than at work. It was annoying as fuck to be sitting there being ignored.

When I finally did get the chance to speak to someone about dropping the charges against Hov, the detective didn't know what I was talking about. Once he finally did find my files and stuff, he gave me some halfhearted speech about how me dropping the charges could lead to further shit in the future and blah, blah, blah. It wasn't that what he was saying was bullshit, but it was just the way that he was saying it. He didn't sound anywhere close to interested in anything that had to do with me or my situation so I was *definitely* read to get my ass up out of there as soon as possible.

Jasheem and I had been in the precinct for hours so when we got out it was around lunch time. I asked him what he wanted to eat and he said a burger. I took him to a diner in the area and we had lunch. He got a burger and fries and I had a chicken salad. When we got back to the hotel, it was a wrap. Jasheem knocked out within a couple of minutes of us getting back inside.

I pulled out my phone and dialed Tamika. I hadn't spoken to her in like two days and I had mad shit to catch her up on. When I got started, she told me to just save the story for in person cause she needed to be face to face with me for this conversation. Within the hour Tamika was knocking on my door.

"Damn, this is a nice hotel," she said as she walked in. "Marco must have some money to be takin care of you like this."

"Hush," I said to her as I closed the door. "I

ain't say nothing about Marco to Jah and I don't want to until I have to," I said.

"My bad," she said. "So, come on. I need to hear this whole story." I checked in on Jah who was still sleeping on the bed. I closed the door so Tamika and I could sit in the little living room area and talk. We took a seat on the arm chairs across from one another.

"Girl, I don't even know where to start," I said to her with a deep sigh. I hadn't really had much time to just sit down and chill out. I hadn't really processed any of the shit that was happening but I still kept going. It was good that Tamika was there cause I just needed to speak to someone out loud and get all that shit off my chest.

"Well you already told me how you ended up here, but what happened after?" she asked me.

"I wish I had a drink...a blunt, somethin'," I said to her. I didn't really smoke like that but at moment I just needed something to make me chill all the way out. "So I invited Marco back to the room last night."

Tamika's eyes got all wide like she was shocked. Then she put her hands over her mouth to cover up the sounds of her own damn screams. I had to remind her that Jah was sleeping in the room.

"Wow sis, that's crazy," she said to me. "I can't believe it. But wait, y'all had sex, right? I'm not just assuming shit am I?"

"Nah, not at all," I admitted to her. I sighed again and shook my head. The look on Tamika's face was exactly how I still felt about the situation; shocked. I had really gone all the way with someone else but even more than that, I enjoyed that shit.

"How was it?" Tamika asked. "How do you feel? Girl this is new for you. Hov done had you on lock for years."

"Girl I know," I said. "It was good. Really good. Marco just…" I trailed off. I had a couple of quick flashback to that morning. It was like I could feel him or something. I knew that they'd come to clean the room but I still smelled him.

"Damn bitch, you got it bad," Tamika said, snapping me from my thoughts.

"Shut up," I said. "But I don't know how to feel. I really don't. You know me Mika, I'm not the type to do something like that. Hov did me

wrong mad times and I never tried to get that
nigga back like this."

"Maybe you not tryin to get back at him,"
Tamika said

"What you mean?" I asked. She was
confusing me.

"I mean...what if this is your way of starting
to leave Hov for good?" Tamika asked.

I just rolled my eyes at her but she kept
going. "Nah, I'm serious Jericka," she said.
"Think about it like this: you did something you
never thought you'd do, right after Hov fucked
up in a big way. This ain't revenge, this is the
universe telling you to leave that nigga. You
think you could've fucked Marco if you ain't see
some kind of future with him? Hell no. Why
you think you ain't cheat on Hov after all the
times he did you dirty?"

As much as I hated to admit it, Tamika did
have a point. "That's true," I said to her. "I just
don't know. I'm just trying to take it slow." I
paused, cause I'd been debating whether or not
to tell Tamika all of it but I just decided to come
clean "I dropped the charges against Hov."

"What? Why the fuck would you do that?"
she asked me. She stood up and started walking

back and forth. She rolled her eyes at me and then sat back down. "Jericka, what's really good with you? Where's your mind at? Why would you drop the charges?"

"He text me, saying he wanted shit to get better for us and all that," I said.

"And you believed him? I can't believe this shit," she said. She just shook her head at me

"Mika, you just gotta trust me. It's different this time," I said to her.

"How?" she asked. She crossed her arms.

"I'm not getting back together with him for one thing. I told him that I was only dropping the charges if he went to rehab and completed the program. I also told his ass that I wouldn't even think about getting back together with him unless he stayed clean for a month straight," I explained to her.

"I mean...that's good I guess," she admitted. "Are you actually thinking about getting back with him?"

"I don't know," I said sadly. "I love him but I feel like I'd be dumb to turn down Marco and everything that he's trying to give me.

"True," said Tamika. "You got a real decision on your hands."

"No I don't," I said. "I ain't got shit to choose. I just need to make sure me and Jah are good. These niggas are gonna be these niggas regardless."

She started laughing. "Ain't that it?"

"I don't know what's gonna happen but I'm just gonna go with the flow in the meantime. I wanna just take it slow with Marco and feel him out. I'll check in with Hov every now and then to see if he's keeping his word but I'm not his babysitter.

"I feel you," she said. "I hope it works out for you. Marco sounds like a good dude. He's got my vote."

"Hush," I said with a laugh. Tamika stopped being a fan of Hov a long time ago. My phone started to ring. It was Marco calling me.

"Hello?" I answered. I waved my hand in Tamika's face and then motioned for her to be quiet. I put the phone on speaker.

"What's good?" Marco's deep voice came through the speaker. "What you up to?"

"Nothing really. I just came back in from getting Jah not too long ago," I said. "What about you?"

"I'm just out here livin' life," he said. "I was

thinking though...what you doin' tomorrow? You wanna go look at some apartments?"

I was surprised by it. He'd mentioned that last night but I didn't think he was being serious. "I'm down," I said to him. "I'm gonna bring Jah too."

"That's cool," he said. "Maybe the three of us can go out for dinner or somethin' after."

"I'd like that," I said.

"Aight, cool," he said. "I gotta run but I'll hit you later on and see what you doing."

"Ok, talk to you later," I said before I ended the call.

Tamika looked impressed. "Damn girl, he tryin' to put you up in an apartment? He's big time for real."

"I know," I said.

"*That's* that kind of man you need to have around your son," she said with approval. "He's about his business for real. And he's trying to prove himself to you. I like him."

I heard everything that Tamika was saying and I knew that I should have been the happiest person in the world. A good man had walked into my life and seemed ready to do shit for me that I need and ain't asking for shit in return but love. He's even willing to take care of my son like his own and what was I doing? I was sitting there still wondering if I was doing the right thing. My mind drifted to Hov and I couldn't help but wonder about what might happen with him.

CHAPTER 6

Hov

Jericka never responded to my text so I just went on about my business. I guess it worked out anyway cause I ain't have no intentions on going to rehab anyway. I knew what I needed to tell her to get back in her good graces. A couple of days went by and I didn't hear from her. I thought about hittin' her up but I decided against it. I wasn't tryin' to get on her nerves.

Kia ended up getting some money that day from somewhere and she and I smoked a couple of times and fucked. The thing was that we'd burned through it all pretty much. I was tryin' to get some more money from somewhere but it hadn't really worked out the way I wanted it to. I wanted more money for drugs. I guessed I could share with Kia if I had enough but I wasn't sure yet.

I hated to admit that shit but I was kind of fucked up over Jericka. My man James had gone to the crib a couple of times and knocked on the door but he never got an answer which I thought was strange. I told him that if he had some free time, I needed him to be on stake out outside the house cause it ain't make no sense for her to not at least be stopping by.

That shit was especially strange cause I'd been driving by her mother's house and hadn't seen her car. I was using Kia's car and neither Ms. Lydia or Jericka knew what it looked like so as long as I ain't get spotted, everything would be cool. I thought that maybe she might have still been using her mother's whip but I saw her mother a couple of times either going to or coming places and she'd been in the car alone each time.

I hated that bitch Tamika but I'd even

driven by her crib a couple of times but I ain't see no sign of Jericka or Jasheem there. It ain't make no sense to me.

I knew the shit was crazy as hell, but I'd even called her strip club a couple of times. I faked like I was a customer looking for his favorite girl and I asked for Jericka under her stripper name. I'd been calling for the last couple of days and asking for her ass and apparently she hadn't been there in almost a week. I thought that she might have told them not to tell me if she was there or not so I took it upon myself to go in there one night lookin' for her. She never came out to dance and when I asked one of the strippers about her, she said the same thing they'd been saying over the phone: Jericka hadn't been to the club in days.

I was buggin' out tryin' to figure out where she was at. She might have been staying at a hotel or something but that shit wouldn't have made no sense. For one thing, her mother wouldn't let her do no shit like that, not when she had that whole house pretty much to herself. Jayson was hardly ever home and she still had spare bedrooms. Another thing was really in the fact that Jericka ain't have no money, at least to my knowledge. Her mother could be fronting the bill for the hotel but I couldn't see that shit either.

I had to admit that the shit did have me tight for real. I wanted to know where the fuck Jericka was with my son. I knew they both had to be safe but I was Jasheem's father and I had a right to know where my son way, regardless of what me and his bitch of a mother were going through. I was sitting on Kia's couch and I felt myself getting more and more pissed off. This was the bullshit that I was talking about when it came to Jericka. I ain't have no time for the games that she was trying to play with me.

"Hov, what's wrong?" Kia asked. I'd been sitting on the couch so deep in my own thoughts that I hadn't even noticed when she came into the house. She had a grocery bag in one hand and her cellphone in the other.

"Nothin'," I said. The look on my face clearly said otherwise though. I was really aggravated that Jericka had pulled this little disappearing act. I thought shit with us was getting better since we spoke and shit but she was acting brand new and shit. I ain't have the time for it.

"Nah, you look over it," she said. "Actually I got something to cheer you up." She put the grocery bag down on the counter that separated the kitchen from the living room. She reached into her purse and pulled out a nice sized baggy of small rocks.

My eyes got all wide and shit. I felt like a nigga possessed cause all the shit I had in my head before had left me. The only thing I was thinking about was the bag in her hand. It was like the shit had hypnotized me or something.

"Yeah, that can make me feel better," I said to her. I stood up and walked over to her. I kissed her on the lips and she dropped the bag on the floor.

After a couple of minutes of kissing and flirting and shit, we were ready to get high. Kia took it upon herself to break it down and light it up. She handed it to me and I smoked it, letting the warm smoke fill my lungs. I tried to hold my breath for as long as I could to make my high be longer but after a couple of seconds I let it out and started coughing.

"Boy please. You can't ghost that smoke," Kia said to me with a laugh. "Hand that shit back."

I took another quick puff and then handed it back to her. I let my head nod back to the back of the couch as I felt the feeling of being so high take me over. I loved the feeling of being like I was high up on the clouds and shit. After a couple more hits Kia fell asleep.

I wanted to take a nap or something but all the shit I'd been thinking about before Kia had come back was still swirling through my mind. I wanted to know where the fuck Jericka was and who she was with. I knew she wouldn't have left the city or nothing like that and she didn't really have any family close enough for her to stay with. I was thinking hard about that shit. I thought about following Ms. Lydia or Tamika but I decided not to cause it wouldn't have made any sense. There was no guarantee that they'd go see her wherever she was at.

"Let me text this broad," I mumbled to myself. Kia was snoring lightly in her sleep so I knew she hadn't even heard me.

I pulled out my phone and went to my

messages with Jericka. I reread my last message and got mad all over again that she still hadn't responded. I made sure that when I typed out my message that I ain't mad or nothin' but in my body I was hot, and not just from the drugs. The nerve of her ass to try and have me out here following her directions and shit. That whole rehab thing had to be a joke.

Yo Jericka, I hope all is well with u. I wanted to hit you up again to see if u could hit me off with the money for me to get to rehab? If so can we meet up so I can get it from u? I still ain't got no money and like I said I'm tryin' to go so that we can get stuff started again. U got me or nah?

I reread the text before I sent it. Yeah, it sounded cool enough. I sent it to her and waited a couple of minutes for her reply. It was the middle of the afternoon so I assumed she wasn't busy. My phone went off after a little bit. I read it and from the first sentence I got annoyed.

Hov I don't know about all that. I wasn't really trying to link with you. Is there some other way for me to give you the money? I can give it to your friend James or something like that.

I rolled my eyes and shook my head. This

bitch had lost her mind. If I wanted someone else to go get the money for me then I'd have said that. Clearly I was trying to meet up with her. Maybe she knew that and that was why she was against, it but I didn't really have the time to deal with her shit. But the more I thought about it, the more I realized that I needed to play the game with Jericka cause it was the only way for me to get what I really wanted.

I feel u. It would be cool if we could link up later on just for the money. It don't have to be a big thing. We can just meet at our house later on. Maybe we can even talk a little bit? I promise I won't touch u and u don't gotta stay there.

I wanted to make sure that I was addressing all of what he concerns might be.

Hov I really don't know. I feel like we should meet in public or something. I wasn't trying to get into the house and talk to you, at least not now.

"Yo, what the fuck is wrong with this bitch?" I asked out loud. I had to have been bugging out when it came to Jericka cause I didn't know she had all this life inside her. If she was in front of me, I probably would've slapped the shit out of her just for tryin to give me all these terms and conditions and shit.

I typed out my response. *Nah, i feel u. I want to make you as comfortable as possible but I wanna show u that I already been working on my change. That's why I brought up us meeting at the house. I also really just wanted to talk to u though cause I wanted to tell u where my head was and hear where yours was. Plus I wanna know how my little man is. :-)*

I read the response once before I sent it to her. I sent it cause I was sure that it would work out in my favor. I was making sure to be as respectful as possible but I wanted her to know that I was really trying. The conversation that I was gonna have with her was different that the one I was describing though.

I get what you saying. I can meet you at the house later to give you some money to get to rehab. I'm not promising that I'll talk but I'll try and listen. I don't want no shit Hov. And Jah ain't comin with me either.

I rolled my eyes. Whatever. I wanted her to bring Jah but I wasn't gonna press the issue with her any further.

Thanks. I really appreciate it. Let me know what time is good for you.

I sent the message to her and decided to take a little nap. My mind had been going a mile a minute for a while now and I was finally feeling better about shit since Jericka's ass finally agreed to meet up with me. It was crazy that she was trying to put me through all that bullshit to see and it was fucked up that she wasn't bringing Jah. I would deal with it though. Jericka had a lesson to learn.

CHAPTER 7

Jericka

The next couple of days went by smoothly. I thought for sure that Jah wouldn't have liked the hotel but he got used to it. He liked that I let him jump on the bed and that I wasn't always telling him to help clean up. I also made sure to take him by my mother's house a lot cause I wanted stuff to be normal to him.

I was going to go by the club and work but Marco had made it clear to me that he wasn't with it, not as long as he was helping me out. He'd come back over later on that night. Jah had woken up from his nap, hung out with Tamika and I, and then tired himself out all over again. By the time Marco came over, Jah was sleeping again.

"Your little man sleep, huh?" Marco asked as he took a seat on the couch in the living room area of the hotel room. He was dressed in a light blue button down shirt a pair of light colored jeans. I greeted him with a long hug. He leaned in and pulled me in tightly. I inhaled his scent.

"Yeah he is," I said. "I wanted him to meet you but it got late so I put him down. I was also thinking that it probably wouldn't be best for you to be here in the morning when he wakes up. I don't wanna send the wrong message."

"Nah, I completely get it," he said as he nodded his head. "I mean...you and your dude or whatever that nigga is just went through this whole thing a few days ago and it ain't gonna look right for you to be laid up with the next nigga."

"Exactly," I said to him. I always told Hov that it was really important to always at least project the right kind of image to Jasheem. I didn't want him to see too much bad and have it shape the way that he goes about living his life. He was already dealing with feelings towards

Hov. I wasn't about to let him see me and Marco kissing or something and have him get some negative thoughts towards me.

Marco and I caught up. He told me about his day and actually went into detail for once He'd spoken to his brother and put more money on his books, even though he didn't need to. He said that he'd stopped by his brothers' baby mother's house and threw some money her way too. I liked that he was able to hold down his whole family.

We talked for a little while longer and when I mentioned to him that I'd been thinking about going to the club at some point that week, he'd made it clear that he wasn't with it at all.

"Nah, why you gotta go back there?" Marco had asked me. He was looking at me with a real serious look in his eyes.

"What you mean, *why?*" I asked him. "I need money and stuff. How else am I gonna get it?" I asked him. Marco was cool and I appreciated everything that he was doing for me but he needed to know that I'd been taking care of me and the people around me for a long ass time. Going back to the club wasn't something that I *wanted* but when it came down to things that I needed, money was at the top of the list.

"I got you," he said to me. "You see all this shit? You thought I was playin' when I said I was gonna help you out?"

I shook my head at him. "Nah, it's nothing like that," I explained. "I just like having my own."

"Look, if you need anything, come to me or don't but that club shit is tired," he said. "I'm not tryin' to tell you what to do but why not just chill out? Take some time off or something like that?"

"And what am I gonna do with the time off?" I asked him.

"Get your shit back together," he said to me. He'd said it like it was the easiest explanation in the world. "I already told you I'd help you find a new crib and shit tomorrow. Just focus on that. Like I said, I don't want you back in the strip club but I can't tell you what to do.

That was a new attitude for sure. I'd been dealing with niggas who thought they could tell me what to do with for the longest. At home, Hov had made it clear that I was supposed to bring him my money for him to spend, and still manage to take care of the bills. At the strip club, dudes wanted you to do all types of Gold medal ass acrobatics and shit just for them to come up off of a dollar. I was tired of being told what to do. It was nice that Marco wasn't trying to control me like other people did.

Marco and I talked about the strip club thing for a little while longer and I decided it probably wouldn't be best for me to go back there, at least not in the near future. We talked for a little while longer that night before he left me and headed to wherever he stayed at.

Tamika had called me one day out of the blue while I was riding around with Jasheem. He and I were just coming back from Walmart. I'd picked up some stuff for my mother and we were driving back to her house when Tamika had called me.

"Hey sis, what's going on?" I said as I answered the phone. I connected her to the phone speaker.

"Hi aunty!" Jasheem said loudly from his car seat in the back.

"Hi baby! Hey sis, what you up to?" Tamkia's loud voice came through the whole car.

"We just came from Walmart, heading back to my mama's house," I said. "What about you?"

"Not a damn thing," she said. "Let's go get a drink somewhere."

"Nah," I said. "I got Jah with me. It would be fine if it was just me but you know Ii don't drink and drive with him in the car." It might have been some backwards ass logic but it was mine.

"I can come pick you up from Ms. Lydia's house," Tamika said. "It's nothing crazy, just something to take the edge off."

"I don't know," I said to her. I wasn't sure why I was feeling so unsure.

"Girl, it's been a couple of days since we seen each other, just come out," she pleaded with me. "All you seen this week is that damn hotel room, your mother and her house, Jah and Marco. What about me? You don't love me no more. You don't got no time for me." She sounded like a little ass kid pleading with their parent.

"You so dramatic," I said to her. I shook my head and smiled in my car. Tamika could be a lot to deal with but she always meant well.

"Does that mean you coming?" She asked me with a laugh.

"We'll be there," I said. "You can come to my mother's house and get us. She ain't even home from work yet."

"Alright, I'll be there in a few," she said.

"Sounds good," I said to her before we got off the phone.

An hour later, Tamika, Jasheem and I were all sitting around the table at a local restaurant. Jah was eating chicken fingers and staring at his iPad, paying Tamika and me no attention at all. I was sipping on a margarita and she was drinking a vodka and cranberry.

"Mmm," she said as she took her first sip. "This shit is good. They put the limes in just the way I like."

"Good," I said. I sipped my margarita, liking it as well. "So what you beep up to?"

"Girl, you know me, just hustling," she said to me. "I'm getting tired of doing hair one to one though. I was thinking about looking into some stuff so I can start a salon."

I nodded my head in approval. "Ooh shit, that sounds good. You should do it."

"I'm looking into it," she said. "It's just a lot

of bullshit behind it and not to mention that I'm gonna need money and shit to make anything happen."

"It's a lot of work but you can do it. This not the first time you mentioned it," I said. "Go for it."

"I will," she said. "How you been? How's your week been? Marco still coming by for them late night visits?" she asked me. I made a face at her and looked at Jasheem. He had his headphones in so he wasn't even paying us any attention at all.

"Shut up," I said. "But yeah, he's come by a couple of times," I told her. Since that first night, Marco had made it a habit of coming over. He still hadn't met Jah cause he'd always been sleeping but it was cool for me to just kick it with him when he came through.

"How's stuff been going with him?" she asked.

"It's just going," I said. "Good, I guess. Nah, it's been going good. I can't even lie. We just been talking and stuff. It's cool to just spend some time getting to know him. I don't let him spend the night but he don't even trip off that shit."

"That's good," Tamika said. "Too many niggas out here by too hard up for pussy so it's nice that the niggas at least knows how to chill out."

"Right," I said. "I just need shit to settle down though. Jah is cool with the hotel. He thinks this shit is an adventure or something but I'm getting over it."

"How'd the apartment search go with Marco?" she asked me.

"Girl, he ain't even do no real research," I said with a laugh. "I think he just thought we'd be able to go places and just see them. I told him that he should find a broker or something."

"Yeah, that's the only way to do it," she said. "Even though they be charging an arm and a leg."

My phone was sitting on the table and I felt it vibrate before Tamika could look up and see who it was that was texting me. I'd never responded to Hov's text asking me for money and it had been a couple of days since so I was sure that's what he was hitting me up for.

"Ooh, a text. Who's it from?" Tamika asked me.

I just laughed nervously. "Marco's just

checking on me," I lied to her. It was Hov asking me about money to get to rehab. I hadn't answered his last message on purpose. I was hoping that if a couple of days went by that he'd either let the idea slip from his head or he'd get the money from somewhere else.

I spent the next ten minutes talking to Tamika and texting Hov. He was getting on my nerves cause he wasn't making it easy on me. I was trying to be reasonable with him but I honestly wasn't trying to see him.

Hov needed to realize that he'd fucked up the way that he did me the last time we'd seen each other. Ain't no way in hell that he should have been thinking that I was just gonna come to the house and chill out and talk to him.

The only reason I even agreed to go was cause he didn't seem like he was gonna let the shit go. I knew Hov and knew how persistent he could be when he wanted and I wasn't trying to get annoyed...not when I was trying to enjoy my time with Tamika.

As we drove back to my mother's house, Tamika and I kept on chopping it up but I didn't tell her about Hov hitting me up, or that I'd agreed to go and meet him later on that day.

I didn't wanna hear her mouth. We'd managed to get through the whole meal and drinks without mentioning Hov at all so I wasn't trying to mess up the vibe. I text him and told him what time I was gonna be able to meet him and he text me back saying he'd be there on time.

She dropped us back at my mother's house and drove off. Jah and I went inside where my mother was in the living room watching TV. She still had on her stuff from work and she looked kind of tired.

"Hey ma," I said as I greeted her. "How was work?"

"It was alright. Where y'all coming from? Thanks for getting the tissue and paper towels for me," she said.

"We were out with Tamika," I said. "Ma, would you mind watching Jah for me for like an hour?"

"Yeah, that's fine," she said. "Where you going?"

"I just have a quick errand to run," I told her. It wasn't a lie. Me meeting up with Hov and giving him the money for rehab was a quick errand. I didn't plan on staying in the house with him for too long.

The closet rehab place was just on the edge of town. It shouldn't have cost too much for him to get there. I put $25 into my purse. That was all the money I was bringing with me. I wasn't bringing more cause I didn't wanna put the temptation out there for him to ask for more. I'd make it clear to him when I saw him that that was all the money I was bringing out with me.

The drive back to my house wasn't too bad. It felt kind of weird to be going back there since It had been a couple of days since I'd been there. Marco had given me some money and I'd just used that to get some new stuff for me and Jah as I needed it. Jah was good on clothes for the most part though. He had almost a whole other wardrobe at my mother's house.

As I drove back to my house, I tried to put myself into the right mindset to deal with Hov and everything that came with him. Hov was on some next level shit and he needed to learn a lesson. The only way that I was gonna get through to him was if I made sure not to give him everything he wanted.

I pulled into the lot outside the complex where we lived. I pulled out my phone and text

Hov, letting him know where I was and asking him where he was. I didn't see his car.

It crossed my mind right before I got out the car that if I wanted to, I could have just not gotten out, went back to the hotel, and just moved on. I didn't owe Hov anything, especially not after what he'd done to me and almost to Jah. I got out of the car and walked up the apartment, not sure of what would be waiting for me on the other side.

CHAPTER 8

Hov

Kia must've been tired as hell cause she slept for forever. Once Jericka finally agreed to meet up with me, I knew I needed to be ready. I really couldn't believe the way that things had changed for me and her. She and I had been on top of the world at one point in time and now I was staying at Kia's house, listening to her ass snore and shit.

Since Kia was sleeping, I knew her ass wouldn't mind me taking another couple of pulls. I inhaled that shit and held it for as long as I could. It burned my throat a little bit but I ain't care too much. She was knocked out so I knew she wouldn't mind if I took some of her stash with me either.

I chilled out for a couple of minutes before I finally got up and headed to take a shower. Jericka finally text me back, telling me what time she'd be at the house. I texted her back saying that it was alright and that I'd see her there.

I headed into the bathroom and took off my clothes. I turned on the shower and found the perfect temperature before I climbed in there. The water was warm but on the inside I was boiling hot.

Standing in the shower, I couldn't help but let my mind wander. I couldn't believe that shit with Jericka. I thought I knew her for sure but now she'd switched up on me. When you know someone the way that I thought I knew Jericka, you ain't really expect too many surprises but she'd really come out of left field with this whole rehab thing again.

Jericka always talked to me about rehab and stuff. I knew that she wanted me to go. I couldn't lie, there were plenty of times that I thought about going myself. Nobody knew that that shit was like though. I had somehow let myself become a joke in the hood. Niggas used to be afraid of me or at least respect me but that all changed when I started getting high.

I remembered the first time I got high. I was at some back alley gambling shit with James. It was high roller shit only. James was someone that I'd only just met at the time. He had his own shit going on, credit card and check scams and shit like that. He was a cool dude and it was him that put me on to using anything other than weed for the first time.

We were at one of the tables in the back and I was there with some of my people and he was there with his. We'd connected with each other cause we were about to do business. That nigga was on some extra flashy shit. He convinced me to sprinkle a little coke on top of my weed cause he said that it just made the high last longer.

Honestly speaking, I knew it was bullshit, but I had always had a curiosity about all that other shit. All those other drugs and shit had always had me wondering what it was about them that made people so addicted to them. From there, the rest was history.

After a while, I started getting high to balance out my lows. Everything just went places it shouldn't have gone. After a while, I'd lost more shit than I could count. Don't get me wrong, I loved Jericka and Jasheem for real, but I missed all the shit I used to have: cars, clothes, sneakers, electronics, all that shit. I kept getting high cause it made me stop missing out on shit that I ain't have no more. But after a while it ended up turning me into some other shit.

I could give Jericka the benefit of the doubt, she really only did want what was best for me, but I knew me better than anyone. I wasn't going to rehab. If I wanted to get clean, I was gonna do it on my own terms, and I wasn't ready for that shit yet so it wasn't. Her asking me to go to rehab before she even thought about getting back with me was some bullshit and the more I stood in that shower, the more pissed off I got just thinking about that shit. She had some fucking nerve, for real. I ain't never once try and put her through no hoops and shit for nothing at all that I gave her.

I got out the shower and got dressed. I made sure that I had everything I needed for Jericka. Kia had gotten up while I was in the shower and moved herself from the couch to the bed. She was sleep there with her back to me. That was good cause the last thing I wanted or needed was for her to roll over and start asking questions.

After I double checked myself in the mirror, I decided to take another hit before I headed out. While I was driving back to my house, I wanted to speed through all the light and shit but I wasn't about to risk getting pulled over, not when I had a date with the most disloyal bitch I'd ever met.

I was fuming as I drove back to our crib. Shit, could I even call it our crib anymore? It felt like so long since we'd been happy in there. It felt like that shit was just another reminder of everything that we ain't have no more. The thing that was fucking me up was the fact that the little that I did have left, Jericka was trying to take from me. I ain't have no one else in the world left besides her and Jasheem, and she was trying as hard as she could to take that little bit away from me.

"Fuck that!" I said as I pulled into a spot outside of our complex. I slammed my hand on the steering wheel a couple of times. I was high as shit but fuck it, that wasn't where my emotions were coming from. Jericka had fucked up and I needed to teacher her a lesson.

I got out the car and went inside the house once I saw that

I waited inside the crib for about fifteen minutes before I saw Jericka get out of her car. The whole time before she came, I felt like I was being haunted or some shit. It felt like I could just feel all these different things just from being in the house. That only made me even more pissed off. Jericka must have left right after our fight because nobody had cleaned up. It was still just as fucked up as when I'd left a few days ago.

I stood to the left of the front door. When Jericka came inside, she wouldn't see me until she closed the door. I patted the front of my pants, glad that I'd decided to grab my piece. Jericka ain't know it I kept a gun hidden in her car just in case we ever needed it. I took that shit out before I gave her the car back and she ain't know no better. When I was getting dressed, I made sure that I brought that shit with me. I didn't plan on using it...but you know how plans can be sometimes.

My heart was beating loudly in my chest and sweat poured down my face. Thinking back on the shit, if I wasn't so high, I would've been nervous. All the drugs going through my body only hyped up my adrenaline. My heart was so loud that I could hear it echoing through the empty apartment. It wasn't until Jericka slid her key in the lock and opened the door that the silence was broken.

"Hov?" She called out. I couldn't see her cause the door was in the way but I could definitely hear her. She'd opened the door but she hadn't walked through it yet. I was waiting for her to come all the way in. "You here?" she called out to me but I ain't answer.

She walked all the way in and turned to close the door behind her. Once she did that, it was a wrap. I reached out and pushed the door shut. She was so surprised she ain't know what to do. She looked up at me and took a couple of steps back, backing up into the wall in the hallway.

"Why the fuck you look so shocked? I told you I was meeting you here," I said.

She was all bright eyed and shit, still surprised. "What the fuck, Hov?" she asked me. "What's wrong with you? Why you hiding out and shit?"

"Don't ask me no questions," I said to her. I could tell by the look on her face that she was starting to figure out that I was high. I knew I had to be looking crazy to her. "How much money you bring?"

"Hov, are you high?" she asked me. She looked like she was a good mix between hurt, scared, and confused.

"Jericka, stop playing with me!" I said loudly. My deep, loud voice filled the apartment and made her jump just a little bit. "How much money did you bring?" I repeated the question louder this time around.

"Relax," she said in a calm way. Her voice might have been calm but I could see from the look in her eyes that she was anything but. "I brought $25 with me, that's it. You could take a cab to rehab from here and still have a couple of dollars left."

"Don't play with me Jericka," I said to her. I wasn't in the mood for her or her games. I was over her for real. Ain't no way in hell that she only left the house with just twenty five fuckin' dollars. She had to know that I was gonna want more than that. "How much money did you bring for real?"

"Hov, I promise you, that's all the money I brought," she said. She sounded like she was telling the truth but who could really be sure.

"Whatever Jericka," I said. "You a fuckin' liar anyway so it don't matter."

"I'm a liar?" She asked. She had the nerve to stand there acting all surprised like she ain't know what I was talking about. She was pissing me off even more.

"Hell yeah you a liar," I said. "I know you got more money than that. Where you been staying?"

"What you talk 'bout?" She played dumb with me. "I'm staying at my mother's house, me and Jah."

I just shook my head. My eyes were on fire and I was having a hard time trying to calm down. "See...there you go lying again. I know you not staying at your mother's house cause I stopped by there and ain't see you. And don't even lie and say you was with Tamika cause that's a lie too," I explained to her. She looked shocked. She definitely wasn't expecting me to know all the shit that I knew. Jericka needed to stop playing with me.

"You been following people?" she asked me.

"Yo, I don't even know you no more. Who the fuck are you? You stalking me now?" She looked pissed off.

"Jericka, don't play with me," I said to her. "Don't try and flip this shit on me. Where you been staying at?"

"At a hotel," she said to me, and she looked even more pissed off. When she spoke again, it seemed like she'd finally gotten her backbone back. "Hov, you need to just chill out."

"What hotel you been staying at Jericka?" I asked her. My voice was flat and dead serious.

"It don't matter," she said.

"I asked what hotel you been staying at?" I repeated to her.

"Hov, don't come at me with this bullshit," she said loudly. "I ain't tellin' you shit. I'm safe and so is Jah and that's all that matters.

"Why won't you tell me?" I asked her. She didn't know it but my patience was running low. I was already at the end of a short fuse when I came in the house and now that she was trying to flip it on me, I wasn't with it at all.

"Cause you got other shit to worry about, Hov," she said. "Go worry about rehab. Go worry about getting and staying clean." She paused and looked me up and down. "Go worry about why I had to hold us down all this time and you ain't been doing shit!"

The worst thing about loving someone is that you know and understand them which means that you understand what makes them tick and what can hurt them the most. Jericka knew the places inside of me that could piss me off the most. She knew every sore spot, every bad thing, and every place that was hitting below the belt. She was definitely hitting me below the belt with that shit and in that moment I wasn't in control of myself. All the anger and frustration that I'd been holding on to seemed to come from nowhere and before I knew it, I'd balled up my fist, walked over to Jericka and punched her in the face.

I was pissed off. My anger mixed with my high was nothing to be played with. I ain't even realize what happened until I saw Jericka on the floor. I'd drawn back my hand hard and let loose with one hard punch. Before she knew what happened or even had a chance to try and fight back, my fist had already connected with the side of her face. I'd hit her hard. She dropped to the floor and I was standing over her trying to figure out what the fuck had just happened.

"Oh shit," I mumbled to myself as I looked down at her on the floor. "Oh shit...what the fuck did I do?" My heart dropped in my chest cause all I could think in my head was that I'd killed her. It was just one punch. That was it. My breathing was so quick and shallow that I thought I was bugging out when I saw her leg move. It happened again and I couldn't believe it.

I must've just knocked her unconscious. She was already starting to slowly move on the floor. I didn't know if she was gaining her consciousness back or what but I came up with a plan, fast.

CHAPTER 9

Jericka

My head was pounding. Nah, it was more than that. Pounding would have felt better. It felt like someone had dried to cut my fucking face off and then halfway through they just decided to give up. My eyes were closed and though it hurt to open then, I slowly peeked through them, trying to figure out what the hell was going on. I needed more than an ibuprofen or aspirin. I needed a whole bag of morphine pumped right into my head or something. The pain was crazy.

My body felt tight and when I tried to stand up, I couldn't. I realized that I was tied to a chair. My hands were tied behind my back with something but I couldn't tell with what. My feet were tied up too.

It all came back to me in a series of flashbacks. I was at my house having a conversation with Hov. He got mad at something that I said and before I knew what had happened, that nigga hit me. The last thing I remembered was him walking over to me in like two steps. I must've pissed him off.

I was so fucking stupid. That was the first thought that came to my mind as I sat there in my living room, tied to a fucking chair, trying to figure out how the hell I was gonna get out of it. Hov was high as hell which meant that I could try and reason with him but it also meant that he had his own way of understanding shit cause he was high. Hov was never himself when he was high but it was so bad that I could tell just from being around him how high he was and that nigga was sky high.

I realized then that I was stupid as hell. Hov had made it clear a bunch of times that he was crazy and I should have been seen the signs before anything happened. I shouldn't have gone to meet him alone. I should have told

someone; Marco, Tamika, my mother, somebody. Instead I'd come out there alone and now
look at what was happening.

The ropes weren't too tight, thankfully, but
they were tight enough for me not to be able to
get out of them. I was trying hard too. I kept
shuffling my feet and hands, trying to loosen up
the knots and shit.

"Oh shit, you up, huh?" Hov walked into
the living room from God only knew where. I
wasn't sure of how long I was out for but he
looked the same, but his eyes were even more
glazed over.

"Hov...Hov…" I was saying his name over
and over again as I tried to get my thoughts
together. It was all just too much for me to deal
with. I would have never imagined in my life
that shit would have turned out this way.
"Hov...untie me. Please. What are you doing?"

"I ain't fucking untying you, you lying
bitch," he said to me. His eyes looked like two
marbles shining in his head. He was clearly too
high for me to try and reason with him but I
wasn't about to try.

"Hov what are you talking about?" I asked
him. I was trying to keep my voice calm, steady,

and in control. I wasn't in a position to bargain with him but I was damn sure gonna try. "I didn't lie to you."

"I went through your purse. I found more money," he said. He held up his hand and in it was $45 dollars.

"Hov...that ain't nothing. Remember I always keep $20 in cash behind my ID in my wallet, just for emergencies?" I explained to him. My mother told me that regardless of anything, I should always have money to get to and from places in case one way wasn't working. She'd always say that a cab can always be caught so I should have cash on my just in case. I tried to get Hov to do it but after he started doing drugs, his ass couldn't keep any money.

"Yeah whatever," he said to me. He reached into the front of his pants and pulled out a gun. It was Hov's gun; cold, jet black metal. I'd seen that gun more times than I could count. He held it in front of him and then looked up at me and then back down at it. He put it on the coffee table between us and I just stayed silent. The gun changed things. I wasn't about to provoke him.

"When the fuck did you become so disloyal,

Jericka?" He asked me. Don't you know that he had the nerve to actually sound hurt? He had the nerve to be calling me disloyal. Hov had cheated on me, disrespected me, and everything else under the son. Now to add insult to injury, he had the fucking audacity to try and tell me that *I* was disloyal?

"Hov, how am I disloyal?" I asked him. It was the only thing for me to say cause I was trying to figure out what he was talking about.

"Jericka don't play stupid with me," he said to me. He sniffled really hard and coughed a couple of times. "You got some nigga paying for the hotel you staying in?"

"What?" I asked. I was scared. Hov was high out of his mind and who knew where that was going to lead us. He'd hit me more times than I could count but this was the first time that things between us had gone so far. I knew he always said that he never wanted to lose his family but this was beyond that.

"So where the fuck you get the money from? Your nigga paying for it, right?" Hov asked. I shook my head. I was sure that he was just fishing for information. That nigga had no proof of Marco. I knew that to be true for sure.

"Hov...please," I pleaded. I'd been trying hard not to let them come but the tears welled up in my eyes. I couldn't believe that this shit was happening. "Ain't no nigga paying for my hotel. You know my mother got money saved. She put it under Jayson's name cause you wouldn't check for it under that."

I'd come up with the lie quickly cause I was trying to just talk my way out of it. I was a nervous wreck though. I could feel the side of my head swelling up. I felt blood mixing with sweat as it trickled down my face. I was trying my hardest to get out of the knots but nothing was working.

"You a fuckin liar Jericka," he said. It was scary to me how calm his voice was just then. I knew that inside his head he had to be going through some real shit but I didn't care about none of that. I just wanted to get out of there safely and get back to my son.

"Hov...whatever I did, I'm sorry for it," I said to him. I held back my tears and tried to steady my voice. I wanted him to believe that I was being sincere, even though I had no idea what he was talking about. "I promise you that I'm sorry. Can we talk about it?"

"Ain't no fuckin talkin 'bout it," he said. "You so fuckin high and mighty and shit. You always lookin' down your nose at me and judging me and shit. You think I don't hear your slick ass comments and shit about how you the one that carries the household? How the fuck you think that makes me feel Jericka?" Hov was speaking so fast that I could barely understand what he was saying. Spit was flying out of his mouth and landing on the table and gun in front of us.

"Hov...please, let me explain," I tried to plead with him. "Yo...Hov...calm down, for real. This don't gotta go no further. We can talk about this and be a family again."

I knew then that I'd fucked up. I guess me mentioning family was the thing that set him off cause he stood up and started pacing back and forth. He was mumbling to himself. I couldn't tell what he was saying but I did catch a couple of words. He mentioned me and Jah. He turned back around to me and started talking so fast that I wasn't even sure he was talking to me.

"You tried to take my family away Jericka. I told you over and over again how much y'all mean to me and you tried to leave me! You tried to take Jah away from me and when I tried to come back you pulled this rehab bullshit? I gotta go to rehab and stay clean just to be your fuckin man again? What type of bullshit is that? Huh?" He paused. He'd been right in my face and speaking loud but not quite yelling.

"Hov, I just want you to be clean," I told him. "I want you to be clean cause I want you to be healthy. I want you to be better again. Remember how much fun we used to have? We ain't have to worry about shit. I was Bonnie and you was Clyde, baby. We can get back on top just like that."

"Nah bitch, you left me when I needed you most," he said. He stared up that pacing shit again and he wasn't looking at me but it was clear he was talking to me. It was some real crazy shit to see how far he'd fallen. He looked like a full blown crackhead who was tweaking out. His movements and shit looked crazy. His face had lost the good looks that he used to be known for. It was now pale and sunken in. His nose was red and starting to turn color.

He paced up and down and kept on talking. "You fucking left, Jericka! You left me when I needed you most. I was only in the fuckin jail for a few days and you was already acting brand new. You ain't answer my calls and shit. Remember how I treated you, bitch?" He paused and sat down on the couch. He crossed his arms and looked at me with hate in his eyes. I didn't recognize him.

"All the shit I did for you. I took care of you. I made sure you was good regardless of anything. You was out there living like a queen and you couldn't handle it when I had a little fuckin problem?"

His mind was all over the place. He was jumping from topic to topic and shit as he spoke like he was just saying whatever thoughts came to his mind.

I didn't think it was possible but I felt like I was watching an explosion happen in slow motion. The more that he spoke, the more Hov got worked up. I could tell by his movements and the way that he was talking that it was only a matter of time before that nigga went off and I was the target of his aggression.

I decided that since it didn't look like I was going to get free that I should use my only bargaining chip. I needed to try and persuade him that I could make things better for him. I didn't think that Hov would kill me but I knew that if he got to that point, he'd probably hit me some more and who knew how bad he would beat me if I couldn't stop him or get away from him.

"Hov," I called. I made sure that my voice was quieter than it was before. I wanted him to have to stop walking and talking to hear me. "Hov...I've been there with you since day one. Since even before there was a day one we been together. I know that we've both fucked up a few times but that's what we do. We can come back from this but only if you want to."

CHAPTER 10

Hov

Jericka was talking a whole lot of shit but I wasn't in the mood to hear it. She kept trying to make excuses for her lack of loyalty and it was starting to piss me off. She needed to learn her place. I'd put up with her and her shit for years and gave her the best of everything. Neither she or her bitch of a mother had to want for anything as long as I was around and this is all I got in return? I was really questioning how I'd known her for this long and was only just then seeing the real her.

"You know what the fuck your problem is,

Jericka?" I asked her. She'd just finished her little stupid ass speech and was sitting in the chair looking pitiful as hell. All that spark and shit she'd had before was gone.

The funny thing was that I almost let her go. I almost just turned around and left the crib and headed back to Kia's house but then I smoked and my thoughts became more clear. I couldn't have just left Jericka on the floor. She would've gotten up and called the cops and I would've been back at square one again. I had to tie her up. It was the only way for me to cover my own ass. Plus, she ain't wanna talk to me before but now she had no choice.

"You not gonna answer?" I asked her. She ain't say shit in response to my question. She was just looking at me, staring me in the eyes with her dark eyes just glaring at me. "Your fuckin' problem Jericka is that you don't got no fuckin respect." I paused and nodded my head at her. It was like a lightbulb was going off in my head. It was all becoming clear to me. "I don't know what the fuck happened but you lost your respect for me and for yourself. You forgot where you came from. I took you up out your mother's house bitch. And when shit went left, what the fuck did you do? You went to the strip club like a fuckin slut."

She was looking at me all surprised and shit like she couldn't believe what I was saying to her. I don't know how the bitch had the nerve to act surprised. It was her doing for sure. She wasn't what I thought she was. Somewhere she got it in her head that it was cool to disrespect me as her man. I always treated Jericka like a queen and she couldn't do the same for me. She had the nerve to hit me with all this shit about Bonnie and Clyde when she was just really a snake.

"How long we been together now? 6? 7 years? You talkin' 'bout it's a rough time and we gonna get through it but how are we gonna do that when you can't even be upfront with me? If this shit was too much you should have left! You stayed here. You can't get mad at me cause you made the choice to stay with me." I sat back down on the coffee table right in front of her. She was only like two feet in front of me. I put my hand on the side of her face and caressed it.

"I can teach you some respect," I said. "You know that right? We ain't fuck in a minute. I can teach you some respect." She looked terrified, which was just what I wanted. I stood up and walked away from her. "Nah, I couldn't do you like that."

"Hov, please, just let me go," Jericka said. "I can just go home. My mother is probably wondering where I am. I told her I'd only be gone for an hour. You know how she is. And she's watching Jasheem."

"Yo, shut the fuck up," I said to her. My voice boomed and she stopped talking. She did have a point. I went back by the door where her phone was and grabbed it from the floor. I headed back into the living room where she was.

"Your passcode still the same?" I asked her. I put the code into her phone and it unlocked. Jericka had no problems with me knowing her passcode. I guess she wanted me to feel secure or something.

It had only been a few hours, barely even three. Nobody had hit her up except her mother asking her where she was. I texted her back saying that what "I" was doing was taking long than expected but that I'd be back sooner than later. Ms. Lydia texted back alright.

"Problem solved," I said to her. I sat down

on the couch and drifted off to sleep. Jericka was making a couple of shuffling noises but I had been up for a while so I had no problems sleeping.

When I got up later on I didn't know what time it was but I could tell that some hours had passed cause it was darker outside than it'd been before. I looked over at Jericka. She was still tied up and was sleeping with her head down. I sat up on the couch and put her phone on the coffee table since I fell asleep with it on my chest.

"Hov," Jericka called out to me. I hadn't even noticed her wake up so it scared me.

"What Jericka?" I asked. My head was a little fuzzy. I was coming down off my high fast, too fast. It felt like I was crashing. I wanted to be up high again. Thankfully I still had more of Kia's stash. I reached into my pocket and pulled it out. I started getting it ready.

"Baby please!" Jericka pleaded with me once she saw me pull the baggie out. "Hov...please don't do it. That shit is messing with your head. You getting all paranoid and shit. We can just move on. I promise I won't tell anyone about

this if we can just move on." She sounded
desperate.

"Whatever Jericka," I mumbled. I was only
halfway paying her any attention. I was thinking
too hard about my next high. I was careful not
to spill a single piece of the precious powder as I
got it ready. I lit the stem and inhaled as much
as I could. I repeated the process a couple more
times and sat back on the couch. The fuzz that
had been making my head cloudy before was
gone. I was feeling better.

It was a long ass night. I ended up having to
text Ms. Lydia and tell her that "I" wouldn't be
home that night and asked if she could keep
Jasheem. She said she didn't mind but she had
work the next morning so I should be there to
pick him up. That bitch Tamika had also text,
telling Jericka that she had really enjoyed their
lunch date earlier and that she shouldn't have to
wait so long to see her favorite people. That shit
only pissed me off even more. Jericka was out
here living the light with lunch dates and shit
while I was slumming it.

Jericka tried a bunch more times to try and
get me to untie her. I had to admit that if she
wasn't anything else, she was committed. She

did everything short of offering me pussy but I wouldn't have been surprised if she'd have done that shit too. She kept telling me we were a family and how sorry she was. I didn't believe her though. Jericka didn't realize that she was making it worse for herself. Every time she tried out a new speech, I just smoked again. By the time the morning had come, she'd stopped talking and I was high as the fucking Man in the Moon.

The following morning, I was up in the living room thinking. I was really trying to figure shit out. I couldn't keep Jericka tied up in the house for too long. Her mother would know something was wrong when she didn't show up to get Jasheem. She was rarely ever late to pick him up and she never just pulled a no show.

I didn't know what my options were though. I could just leave her in the house and leave. Somebody would come by in a couple of days. I scratched that from my mind though cause there was always the chance that no one would come by for a long time. I couldn't call the cops and tell them where she was without implicating myself.

"Shit…" I mumbled to myself. Jericka looked up at me. "Shit, shit, shit."

"What?" she asked me. She was looking at me with confusion all over her face

"Nothing," I said. "None of your business."

"How much longer you think this shit is gonna go on for, Hov? You can't keep this up forever," she said. "Somebody gonna come looking for me."

"And your mother thinks you'll be at her house soon to come and pick up Jasheem," I said. "Shut the fuck up. I got this."

Her phone went off. I looked at it, expecting it to be a text from Ms. Lydia asking her where Jericka was since it was close to the time that she was supposed to be there but it wasn't. The phone was locked but I looked at the name on the screen.

"Who the fuck is Marla?" I asked. Whoever Marla was, she'd called mad times and had texted a few times too. I thought that she was just one of Jericka's girlfriends or something but the bitch was too persistent. She'd been hitting her up like she was her bitch or something.

"Why?" Jericka asked. All that mouth. I couldn't figure out how she still had all that mouth. She was tied to a chair and still managed to be a pain in my ass.

"Why the fuck she keep calling and texting you?" I asked her. The look on her face was blank. I didn't know if that was a good thing or a bad thing though. As I stared at her I couldn't help but realize that she looked bad. Her hair was matted. The side of her face was swollen where I'd hit her before. Blood had dried on her face and her shirt.

"She's some bitch from the club that I work with," she said. "She and I were supposed to hang out yesterday so she's probably wondering where I was."

It might have sounded like something that was believable but I knew that Jericka couldn't be trusted. I scrolled up through the text message conversation and saw some shit that ain't look right. Her and whoever this "Marla" person were talked more than normal. They spoke more than she spoke to Tamika or her mother. She'd also sent her all types of texts and shit asking shit like:

R u ok?

What's good Jericka? I stopped by the hotel when you ain't pick up. U good?

Wya? Why you not responding. I'm a lil worried. Hit my line.

I wasn't a private investigator or anything like that but whoever Marla was, I doubted she was some bitch from the strip club, if it was even a she at all. I wanted to believe Jericka, I really did, but she ain't give me no reason to. She could have just been open and honest with me but once again she'd chosen the bad route. She'd lied to me yet again now she had to be taught some respect for real.

"See this the shit I be talking about. You out here lying to me about shit for what? You and this Marla bitch sure are close. What the fuck is all this? She hitting you up asking you are you alright and shit. She stopped by the hotel to check on you apparently. It's something fishy goin on here," I said.

I pulled back my hand and stretched out my hand. I slapped Jericka hard across the face. She started to cry and then started screaming loudly. I wrapped my hand around her neck and squeezed hard, choking her.

"Shut the fuck up!" I said to her through clenched teeth. I didn't need all that noise and shit attracting somebody. She finally quieted down.

"You a fucking lying whore! Who the fuck is Marla?" I asked before slapping her again. I was gonna get the truth out of Jericka one way or another.

CHAPTER 11

Jericka

I f you would have told me yesterday morning that when I woke up that this was what I was in for, I would have told you that you were a liar. I thought for sure that I knew Hov. When you're with someone for as long as we were, you learn their habits and you learn what someone is gonna do even before they do it. But I guess you don't really know anyone unless you put them into special circumstances.

It was now the second night that I'd been tied to the chair. It wasn't a laughing matter but I felt like a shorty from a Lifetime movie or something like that. My drug addict ex-boyfriend, who people had told me to leave on mad occasions, had tied me up and was beating the shit out of me. It was something worthy of a movie.

When he'd gone through my phone, I had already expected Hov to ask about "Marla." I knew that the text thread had to be close to the on my phone since we spoke often. Marla was the name that Marco was saved under. I decided to save it that way cause I didn't need anyone to know who I was texting. I wouldn't have to answer any questions or anything if another chick was calling me or hitting me up. People would just assume that it was a girlfriend of mine.

The beating that Hov had given me earlier in the day when asking about Marla had been a lot to deal with. It was like he was just taking his rage out on me. I couldn't see a mirror afterwards but I knew that I had to look bad cause my face felt horrible. I was more emotional than I'd been in a long time. This was beyond me just feeling mad at him. This was life and death. Hov had proved to me that the drugs had taken what was left of his mind. Every time I watched him get high, I saw more and more of him slip away. In the moments before he smoked, he was kind of clear but the drugs were a battery in his back, hyping him back up.

To add insult to injury, when I had to go to the bathroom, Hov had made it clear that I wasn't doing it without his help. He stood me up and walked me to the bathroom. Once we got inside, he pulled down my pants and sat me on the toilet. I had to beg him to go stand outside after I reminded him that I was still tied up and couldn't do anything to him. I couldn't even wipe my own ass because of the ties around my hands.

When I was in the bathroom, I managed to take a look at myself in the mirror. I looked bad, worse than ever. My face was all bruised up. My eyes and lips were swollen. I looked like exactly what I'd been through.

He said that he was gonna be in the living room and that he was tired of my speeches so he was moving me into the bedroom. He picked me up, chair and all, and moved me into our bedroom. He sat me next to the bed and turned the TV on, putting on the news. He'd been wearing a button down shirt. He took it off and laid it next to me on the bed. My heart sped up cause he didn't realize what he'd just done.

"If I hear any fucking noise, it's gonna be a problem," Hov said to me. "Look, I'm tryin' to be nice to you. I even turned the TV on."

I'd learned better than to say anything to him. I just nodded at him. He leaned down to me, gun in hands and pressed it to my neck. "A fuckin' problem," he said to me in a menacing tone of voice. He turned and walked out the room, wearing just his wife-beater and leaving his other shirt behind. I said a silent prayer, and waited.

He left the room but then came back in a couple of minutes later with something in his hand. It was a pair of Jasheem's socks.

"On second thought," Hov said. He took the socks, tied them together and tied them around my mouth, gagging me. "I can't trust you."

An hour or two went by and it was night time again. I almost thought that Hov left but I was closer to the front door than he was. I would have heard him leave. I could hear the TV on in the living room but I didn't hear any movement. I assumed that he was sleeping.

Hov had put my cellphone in the pocket of the shirt that he was wearing earlier. When he took it off, my phone was still in the pocket. He was so high that he must not have realized it. I waited and waited but he never came back for it.

I tried to scoot over it and I managed to do it without Hov coming back into the room. My back was facing the bed after I shifted myself to make me move. I pulled grabbed the shirt from the bed since it was hanging half way of. I pulled it hard and it fell to the floor. My phone fell out and landed right on top of it.

I was trying hard to pick it up off the floor somehow but It wasn't working. I was about to give up when I thought I heard something. I thought I heard a knock at the door. It was almost ten o'clock at night. Who the hell would be knocking on the door that late?

"Jericka...you home?" I heard the voice from the other side of the door and thought I was bugging out. It was Marco knocking.

He knew where I lived cause I'd pointed it out to him one time when he and I were driving around. We happened to be in the area and I pointed out my door to him cause it was one of the outward facing ones. I guessed he'd come looking for me.

I wanted to call out to him but the gag was in my mouth. I wanted to scream to him that I was inside and I almost did but then common sense kicked in. I couldn't call out to him with Hov sleeping in the living room. He would wake up and come running. I was pretty sure that Marco could take Hov but Hov had that gun and I didn't want Marco to get shot.

I felt like my time was running out so I had to spring into action. My phone was only a few feet away from me on the floor. I just needed to get it in my hands somehow.

That was when the thought occurred to me that I didn't actually have to get it in my hands. I just had to be able to use it.

I was wearing sneakers so my feet weren't free. However, I'd been spending hours trying to get free so I'd at least loosened the ropes enough for me to get them a little free. I shuffled my feet back and forth. I just needed to get one shoe free.

I'd been moving my feet back and forth for forever, shuffling them trying to get the ropes to loosen up when finally I managed to pull one leg all the way out of the ropes. I stepped on the back of one shoe with the other and pulled it off. I stepped on the front of my sock and pulled my foot all the way out. I wiggled my toes, glad that they were free and God willing I would be too.

Marco had stopped knocking a minute or two ago but I knew that once I text him he'd come back. I used my bare foot to unlock my phone and open my text messages. I thought it wouldn't work but it worked fine. I went to the messages and typed out a message using my foot.

Help. trapped in my house. Heard u knocking. Can't get free. Hov sleep.

My heart was pounding in my chest, making my nerves worse than they'd been earlier in the day. I kept trying to listen out for Hov. If he woke up and was headed for me I needed to know. I didn't think I had too much to fear though cause he'd smoked so much that he was probably crashing. I'd seen him do it before. He could sleep for longer than a day when he was like that.

I sent the message to Marco and just waited for something...anything to happen.

That was when I heard it. Marco must have gotten my text cause I could hear someone trying to break down the front door. There was a loud crash and then I heard footsteps. I felt myself become overcome with joy. I was so happy that I ain't know what to do with myself. If I could have called out, I would have.

"Jericka!" Marco's voice called out to me. I tried yelling but it only came out as loud hums. I stomped my feet on the floor, making as much noise as possible to let him know where I was. A moment later he walked into the room.

Marco was wearing a pair of sweatpants and a white t-shirt but at that minute he should have been wearing a superhero costume cause that's what he was to me right then and there. He walked up to me and untied the gag.

"Yo...what the fuck happened?" Marco asked. His eyes looked like flames. He was angry. I wanted to keep it together but I couldn't. I cried as he undid the ties on me. "Are you good? Can you walk?"

"I'm alright. I can walk," I said to him. He let me all the way free and though I hadn't stood up all the way in a while, I felt alright. I stood and walked around in a circle. My legs felt a little heavy but it was nothing I couldn't handle.

I wrapped my arms around Marco and hugged him tightly. He held me in his arms for a little bit before taking a step back and looking at me. "Where the fuck is that nigga?" he asked me.

"The living room," I said. I pointed down the hall towards where it was.

I walked down the hallway behind Marco. It seemed like he was on fire. His anger was coming off of him in waves. He walked through the house with confidence like he owned the place. He walked into the living room, reached behind him into the string on his sweats and pulled out his gun from under his shirt. I was afraid that he might shoot Hov but he didn't. He held the gun in his hand and came down hard on Hov's head, pistol whipping the shit out of him.

"What the fuck?" Hov yelled out in pain. He stood and grabbed his head in the spot where Marco had just hit him at. A knot was already forming in his head. He looked up and saw me, then saw Marco and the gun in his hands.

"What's good pussy?" Marco asked. He

handed the gun to me and picked up the one from the coffee table that Hov had never moved.

"Who the fuck are you?" Hov asked.

"Ask my bitch who I am," Marco said and pointed to me.

It almost wasn't fair and I almost felt bad for Hov. Marco had beat the shit out of him. He'd gone after him right after he spoke and just beat Hov to a pulp. His hands were shaking by the time he was done. He walked over to me, grabbed the gun and pointed it at Hov.

"No!" I said. Hov was lying on the floor looking worse than he. He was covered in blood and all bruised up. His left hand was all fucked up from him trying to fight back. Marco was standing over him, clearly ready to pull the trigger but I stopped him.

"He's not worth it," I pleaded with Marco. His eyes had been focused on Hov but he turned and looked at me.

"I'm only not killing you cause of her nigga," Marco said. "Next time you might not be so lucky pussy." He spit on Hov before we turned to leave.

We got outside and Marco made it clear that he wasn't playing games with me anymore.

He said we had three stops to make; the hospital so I could get checked up, my mother's house so I could pick up Jasheem, and then to his house. He said we could figure out everything the next day but he wasn't gonna feel safe with me being anywhere else. I couldn't even argue.

Hov

"Kia...come get me...nah, nah...just come one. Yeah...I'm at my spot. Come now," I said before I hung up the phone.

That pussy ass dreadhead nigga had fucked with the wrong one. I was right all along. Jericka was fucking whore which was why she had her new nigga come and get her. It was alright. I had something for her.

Find out what happens next in part four

of When You Can't Let Go! Available Now!

To find out when Mia Black has new books available, **follow Mia Black on Instagram: @authormiablack**

WHEN YOU CAN'T LET GO 4

The harder Hov tries to get his family back, the more difficult it is for Jericka to move forward with Marco. Complicating matters, she and Hov have a child together. It becomes increasingly impossible to shut one man out completely and embrace a new love entirely when there's so much at stake and so much history to contend with.

Hov's showing no sign of slowing down. Now, Jericka has to wonder how much more will Marco put up with before he decides she's not worth the struggle.

Find out what happens in part four of When You Can't Let Go!

Follow Mia Black on Instagram for more updates: @authormiablack

CPSIA information can be obtained
at www.ICGtesting.com
Printed in the USA
LVHW081423140520
655613LV00018B/1669